Off We Go!

Beverley Abramson

Tundra Books

Published in Canada by Tundra Books,
481 University Avenue, Toronto, Ontario M5G 2E9

Published in the United States by Tundra Books of Northern New York,
P.O. Box 1030, Plattsburgh, New York 12901

Library of Congress Control Number: 2005923899

Library and Archives Canada Cataloguing in Publication

Abramson, Beverley
        Off we go! / Beverley Abramson.

ISBN 0-88776-728-1

        1. Human locomotion – Juvenile literature. I. Title.

QP301.A16 2006   j612.7'6   C2005-901734-1

We acknowledge the financial support of the Government of Canada through the Book
Publishing Industry Development Program (BPIDP) and that of the Government of Ontario
through the Ontario Media Development Corporation's Ontario Book Initiative. We further
acknowledge the support of the Canada Council for the Arts and the Ontario Arts Council
for our publishing program.

ONTARIO ARTS COUNCIL
CONSEIL DES ARTS DE L'ONTARIO

Printed in China

1 2 3 4 5 6   11 10 09 08 07 06

Dedication

To my loving mother, for exemplifying interminable vim and vigor; my children,
for their encouragement, enthusiasm, and wisdom; my supportive brother,
sister, and friends; and, above all, to my grandchildren for their infectious smiles,
boundless energy, inspiration, and patience, especially in front of the camera.

Acknowledgments

Although I was behind the camera, there were a lot of people behind me
who deserve my heartfelt thanks: all the children who leaped and soared for
me and their patient parents; Brent Kitagawa for creating the exquisite prints;
Kong Njo for his artistic direction and design; my innovative publisher
and editor, Kathy Lowinger, for inviting me to give life to her imaginative
concept and for her guidance throughout the project; and my dear friend
Barbara Simmons for her unfailing ingenuity and vision.

Fly

Kick it high

Skip

Take
a trip

Hop

Never stop

Twirl

Take
a whirl

Stroll

Watch me roll

Mish-mash

Splish splash

Teeter

Totter

Fling it

Swing it

Tumble

Never stumble

Heave-ho

Toe
over
toe

Off we go!